This book is dedicated to the many people of color
whose pioneering achievements have often been erased
from our history books.
Your perfect gifts of innovation and ingenuity inspire us all!

RAZORBILL

An imprint of Penguin Random House LLC, New York

First published in the United States of America by Razorbill, an imprint of Penguin Random House LLC, 2021

Visit us online at penguinrandomhouse.com.

Library of Congress Cataloging-in-Publication Data is available.

ISBN 9780593203903

Printed in the United States of America
PC

1 3 5 7 9 10 8 6 4 2

Design by Kristin Boyle & Maria Fazio
Text set in Sabon LT Std

THE PERFECT GIFT

A JINGLE JANGLE STORY

LYN SISSON-TALBERT & DAVID E. TALBERT

ILLUSTRATED BY ASHLEY EVANS

RAZORBILL

Once upon a time there was a family of inventors. Journey, Jessica, and Jeronicus: three generations who could pull numbers out of the air, who could make magic from science. And the greatest of their inventions was . . .

The Buddy 3000!

Buddy was new to the world, and the world was new to him! After all, he'd been turned on for the very first time YESTERDAY.

Everything was fascinating to Buddy!

How time
only moved in
one direction.

Cats' whiskers.

Northern Lights.

Spoons.
(Especially spoons.)

Buddy was full of questions. Questions like . . . What is snow?

Is "3000" my last name?

Why don't dogs purr?

What is a rainbow?

More questions like . . .

Who made me?

Journey answered in unison
with her mother and
her grandfather:

"We all did!"

"You see," explained Journey: "Mom designed you."

"Grandpa J. built you."

"And I put the last pieces together, because I believed!"

"An entire family made you."

Buddy loved this answer. He especially liked the part where Journey said "family." It made his brass bearings brighten with joy.

"Next question," he asked. "What is Christmas?"

And so Journey showed Buddy Christmas. She showed him Christmas trees. She showed him family dinners, and snowball fights. She showed him sweet potato casserole and stockings by the fire. She showed him the Christmas spirit of giving and sharing. She showed him Christmas presents—

"Oh no!" Journey cried.
She'd just realized something terrible.
It was Buddy's very first Christmas . . .
but he didn't have a present!

Journey decided to find Buddy the perfect gift. But she had no idea what a robot even liked.

"What's your favorite food?" Journey asked Buddy.
"Music," Buddy answered.

"What's your favorite color?"
"Curiosity," Buddy replied.

"What's your favorite toy?"
"Gravity," Buddy explained.

This was all very interesting information,
but it didn't help Journey very much.

So Journey went to her mother. "What's the best present you ever received?" she asked. Jessica thought about it for a while.

"The best present I ever received," she said, "was something I always wanted but didn't know I had."

Journey asked her grandfather too. "The best present I ever received," he said, "was something I already had but didn't know I wanted."

"That's it! That's it!" Journey shouted. The perfect gift for Buddy was something he'd always wanted, and something he already had!

And Journey knew exactly what it was:

A Family!

Through Cobbleton's storefront names in the film *Jingle Jangle: A Christmas Journey*, we celebrate the ingenuity and invention of those African Americans who came before us.

Listed below are a few of those included in the film. See if you can find them when you watch the movie!

Store Name: A.M. Woods Confectioner
Named After: Pastor Annie Mae Woods
Notable Achievement: One of the founding pastors of Washington, DC's Pentecostal movement. But to her great-grandson David E. Talbert, the writer and director of *Jingle Jangle*, she pioneered a form of unconditional love and humanity that remains the cornerstone of his work to this very day.

Store Name: Sisson Arms
Named After: Dr. Lonnie Sisson
Notable Achievement: The first African American optometrist licensed in the state of Nevada. But to his daughter, Lyn Sisson-Talbert, producer of *Jingle Jangle*, this is a way to honor her late father's legacy and carry on his adage, "Anything is possible with commitment and hard work."

Store Name: Tharpe's & Co. Music
Named After: Sister Rosetta Tharpe
Notable Achievement: Credited as being the "Godmother of Rock & Roll," whose blend of gospel, blues, and electric guitar distortion was extremely important to the origins of rock 'n' roll.

Store Name: M.M. Daly Chemist
Named After: Marie Maynard Daly
Notable Achievement: The first African American woman with a PhD in chemistry.

Store Name: Parsons Hardware
Named After: James A. Parsons, Jr.
Notable Achievement: Conducted research on how to stop metals from rusting, which led to the development of stainless steel.